WISE QUOTES: MARK TWAIN

(423 MARK TWAIN QUOTES)

Vol. 1

Rowan Stevens

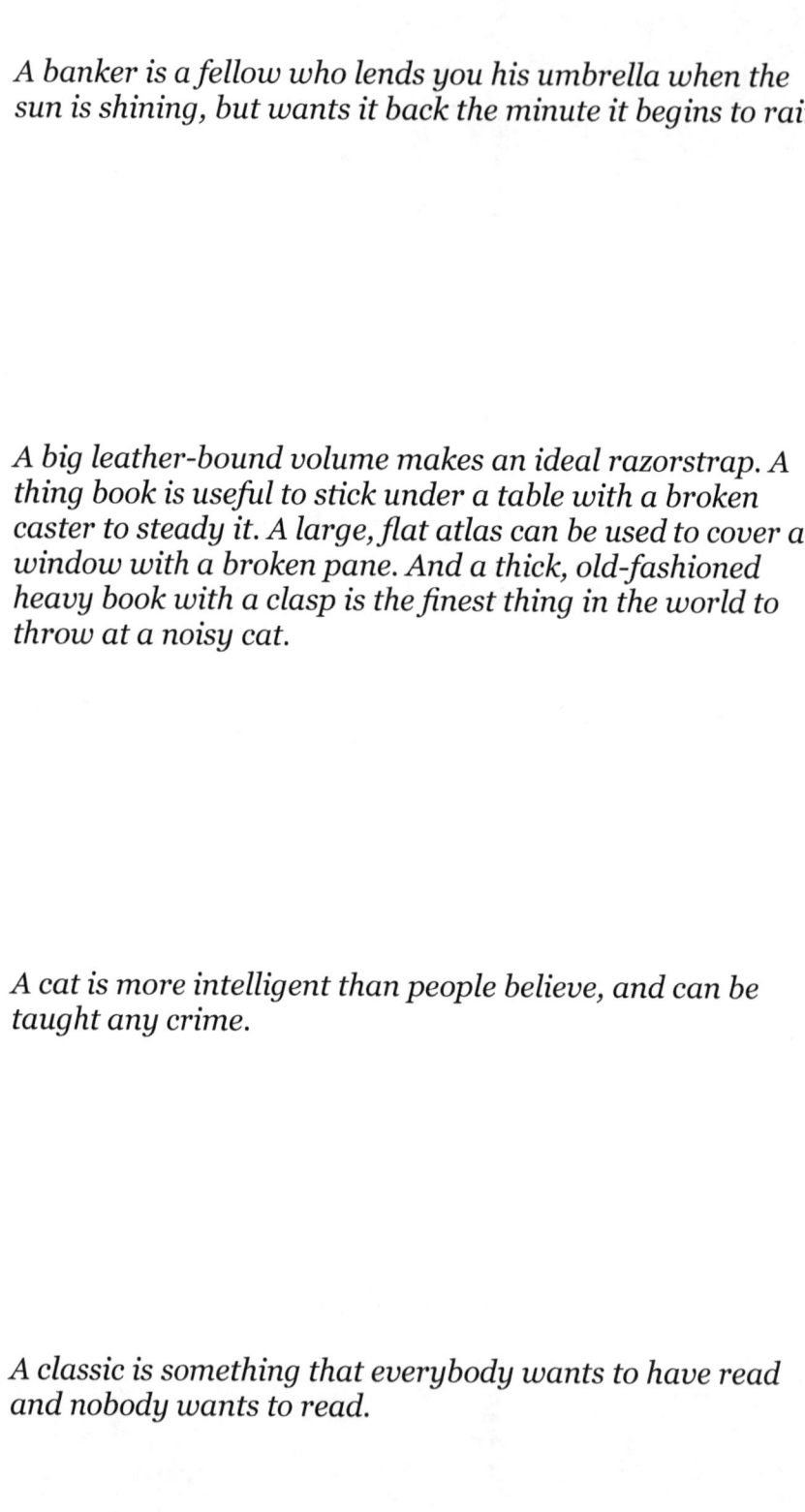

A banker is a fellow who lends you his umbrella when the sun is shining, but wants it back the minute it begins to rain.

A big leather-bound volume makes an ideal razorstrap. A thing book is useful to stick under a table with a broken caster to steady it. A large, flat atlas can be used to cover a window with a broken pane. And a thick, old-fashioned heavy book with a clasp is the finest thing in the world to throw at a noisy cat.

A cat is more intelligent than people believe, and can be taught any crime.

A classic is something that everybody wants to have read and nobody wants to read.

A clear conscience is the sure sign of a bad memory.

A few fly bites cannot stop a spirited horse.

A gentleman is someone who knows how to play the banjo and doesn't.

A God who could make good children as easily a bad, yet preferred to make bad ones; who could have made every one of them happy, yet never made a single happy one; who made them prize their bitter life, yet stingily cut it short; who gave his angels eternal happiness unearned, yet required his other children to earn it; who gave is angels painless lives, yet cursed his other children with biting miseries and maladies of mind and body; who mouths justice, and invented hell--mouths mercy, and invented hell--

mouths Golden Rules and forgiveness multiplied by seventy times seven, and invented hell; who mouths morals to other people, and has none himself; who frowns upon crimes, yet commits them all; who created man without invitation, then tries to shuffle the responsibility for man's acts upon man, instead of honorably placing it where it belongs, upon himself; and finally, with altogether divine obtuseness, invites his poor abused slave to worship him!

A half-truth is the most cowardly of lies.

A home without a cat — and a well-fed, well-petted and properly revered cat — may be a perfect home, perhaps, but how can it prove title?

A lie can travel half way around the world while the truth is putting on its shoes.

A man cannot be comfortable without his own approval.

A man is accepted into a church for what he believes and he is turned out for what he knows.

A man is never more truthful than when he acknowledges himself a liar.

A man who is not born with the novel-writing gift has a troublesome time of it when he tries to build a novel. I know this from experience. He has no clear idea of his story; in fact he has no story. He merely has some people in his mind, and an incident or two, also a locality, and he trusts he can plunge those people into those incidents with interesting results. So he goes to work. To write a novel? No--that is a thought which comes later; in the beginning he is only proposing to tell a little tale, a very little tale, a six-page tale. But as it is a tale which he is not acquainted with, and can only find out what it is by listening as it goes along telling itself, it is more than apt to go on and on and on till it spreads itself into a book. I know about this, because it has happened to me so many times.

A man's character may be learned from the adjectives which he habitually uses in conversation.

A mighty porterhouse steak an inch and a half thick, hot and sputtering from the griddle; dusted with fragrant pepper; enriched with little melting bits of butter of the most impeachable freshness and genuineness; the precious juices of the meat trickling out and joining the gravy, archipelagoed with mushrooms; a township or two of tender, yellowish fat gracing an out-lying district of this ample county of beefsteak; the long white bone which divides the sirloin from the tenderloin still in its place.

A person that started in to carry a cat home by the tail was getting knowledge that was always going to be useful to him, and warn't ever going to grow dim or doubtful.

A person who won't read has no advantage over one who can't read.

A person with a new idea is a crank until the idea succeeds.

A successful book is not made of what is in it, but what is left out of it.

Action speaks louder than words but not nearly as often.

Adam was but human—this explains it all. He did not want the apple for the apple's sake, he wanted it only because it was forbidden. The mistake was in not forbidding the serpent; then he would have eaten the serpent.

After all these years, I see that I was mistaken about Eve in the beginning; it is better to live outside the Garden with her than inside it without her.

Against the assault of laughter, nothing can stand.

Age is an issue of mind over matter. If you don't mind, it doesn't matter.

Ah, if he could only die temporarily!

Ah, that shows you the power of music, that magician of magician, who lifts his wand and says his mysterious word and all things real pass away and the phantoms of your mind walk before you clothed in flesh.

All I care to know about a man is that he is a human being...
he can't be any worse.

All kings is mostly rapscallions, as fur as I can make out.

All men have heard of the Mormon Bible, but few except the
elect have seen it, or, at least, taken the trouble to read it. I
brought away a copy from Salt Lake. The book is a curiosity
to me, it is such a pretentious affair, and yet so slow, so
sleepy; such an insipid mess of inspiration. It is chloroform
in print. If Joseph Smith composed this book, the act was a
miracle — keeping awake while he did it was, at any rate.

All right, then, I'll go to hell.

All you need in this life is ignorance and confidence; then success is sure.

Always acknowledge a fault. This will throw those in authority off their guard and give you an opportunity to commit more.

Always do what is right. It will gratify half of mankind and astound the other.

An honest politician is an oxymoron.

And what does it amount to? said Satan, with his evil chuckle. Nothing at all. You gain nothing; you always come out where you went in. For a million years the race has gone on monotonously propagating itself and monotonously reperforming this dull nonsense--to what end? No wisdom can guess! Who gets a profit out of it? Nobody but a parcel of usurping little monarchs and nobilities who despise you; would feel defiled if you touched them; would shut the door in your face if you proposed to call; whom you slave for, fight for, die for, and are not ashamed of it, but proud; whose existence is a perpetual insult to you and you are afraid to resent it; who are mendicants supported by your alms, yet assume toward you the airs of benefactor toward beggar; who address you in the language of master to slave, and are answered in in the language of slave to master; who are worshiped by you with your mouth, while in your heart--if you have one--you despise yourselves for it. The first man was hypocrite and a coward, qualities which have not yet failed in his line; it is the foundation upon which all civilizations have been built. Drink to their perpetuation! Drink to their augmentation! Drink to-- Then he saw by our faces how much we were hurt, and he cut his sentence short and stopped chuckling...

Anger is an acid that can do more harm to the vessel in which it is stored than to anything on which it is poured.

Any emotion, if it is sincere, is involuntary.

Anyone who can only think of one way to spell a word obviously lacks imagination.

April 1. This is the day upon which we are reminded of what we are on the other three hundred and sixty-four.

Be careless in your dress if you must, but keep a tidy soul.

Be good and you will be lonesome.

Be respectful to your superiors, if you have any.

Books are for people who wish they were somewhere else.

Broad, wholesome, charitable views of men and things can not be acquired by vegetating in one little corner of the earth all one's lifetime.

But death was sweet, death was gentle, death was kind; death healed the bruised spirit and the broken heart, and gave them rest and forgetfulness; death was man's best friend; when man could endure life no longer, death came and set him free.

But who prays for Satan? Who in eighteen centuries, has had the common humanity to pray for the one sinner that needed it most, our one fellow and brother who most needed a friend yet had not a single one, the one sinner among us all who had the highest and clearest right to every Christian's daily and nightly prayers, for the plain and unassailable reason that his was the first and greatest need, he being among sinners the supremest?

By trying we can easily learn to endure adversity – another man's, I mean.

Censorship is telling a man he can't have a steak just because a baby can't chew it.

Choosing not to read is like closing an open door to paradise.

Civilization is a limitless multiplication of unnecessary necessaries.

Classic - a book which people praise and don't read.

Clothes make the man. Naked people have little or no influence on society.

Comparison is the death of joy.

Conservatism is the blind and fear-filled worship of dead radicals.

Continuous improvement is better than delayed perfection.

Courage is resistance to fear, mastery of fear - not absence of fear.

December is the toughest month of the year. Others are July, January, September, April, November, May, March, June, October, August, and February.

Distance lends enchantment to the view.

Do something everyday that you don't want to do; this is the golden rule for acquiring the habit of doing your duty without pain.

Do the thing you fear the most and the death of fear is certain.

Don't go around thinking the world owes you a living. It was here first.

Don't part with your illusions. When they are gone you may still exist, but you have ceased to live.

Don't say the old lady screamed. Bring her on and let her scream.

Don't use a five-dollar word when a fifty-cent word will do.

Don't wake up a woman in love. Let her dream, so that she does not weep when she returns to her bitter reality.

Don't go around saying the world owes you a living. The world owes you nothing. It was here first.

Don't you know what that is? It's spring fever. That is what the name of it is. And when you've got it, you want—oh, you don't quite know what it is you DO want, but it just fairly makes your heart ache, you want it so!

Drag your thoughts away
from your troubles...
by the ears, by the heels,
or any other way you can manage it.

Drawing on my fine command of language, I said nothing.

Each of you, for himself or herself, by himself or herself, and
on his or her own responsibility, must speak. It is a solemn
and weighty responsibility and not lightly to be flung aside
at the bullying of pulpit, press, government or politician.
Each must decide for himself or herself alone what is right
and what is wrong, which course is patriotic and which isn't.
You cannot shirk this and be a man, to decide it against your
convictions is to be an unqualified and inexcusable traitor. It
is traitorous both against yourself and your country.
Let men label you as they may, if you alone of all the nation
decide one way, and that way be the right way by your
convictions of the right, you have done your duty by yourself
and by your country, hold up your head for you have
nothing to be ashamed of.

Eat a live frog first thing in the morning and nothing worse will happen to you the rest of the day.

Education consists mainly of what we have unlearned.

Education: that which reveals to the wise, and conceals from the stupid, the vast limits of their knowledge.

Education: the path from cocky ignorance to miserable uncertainty.

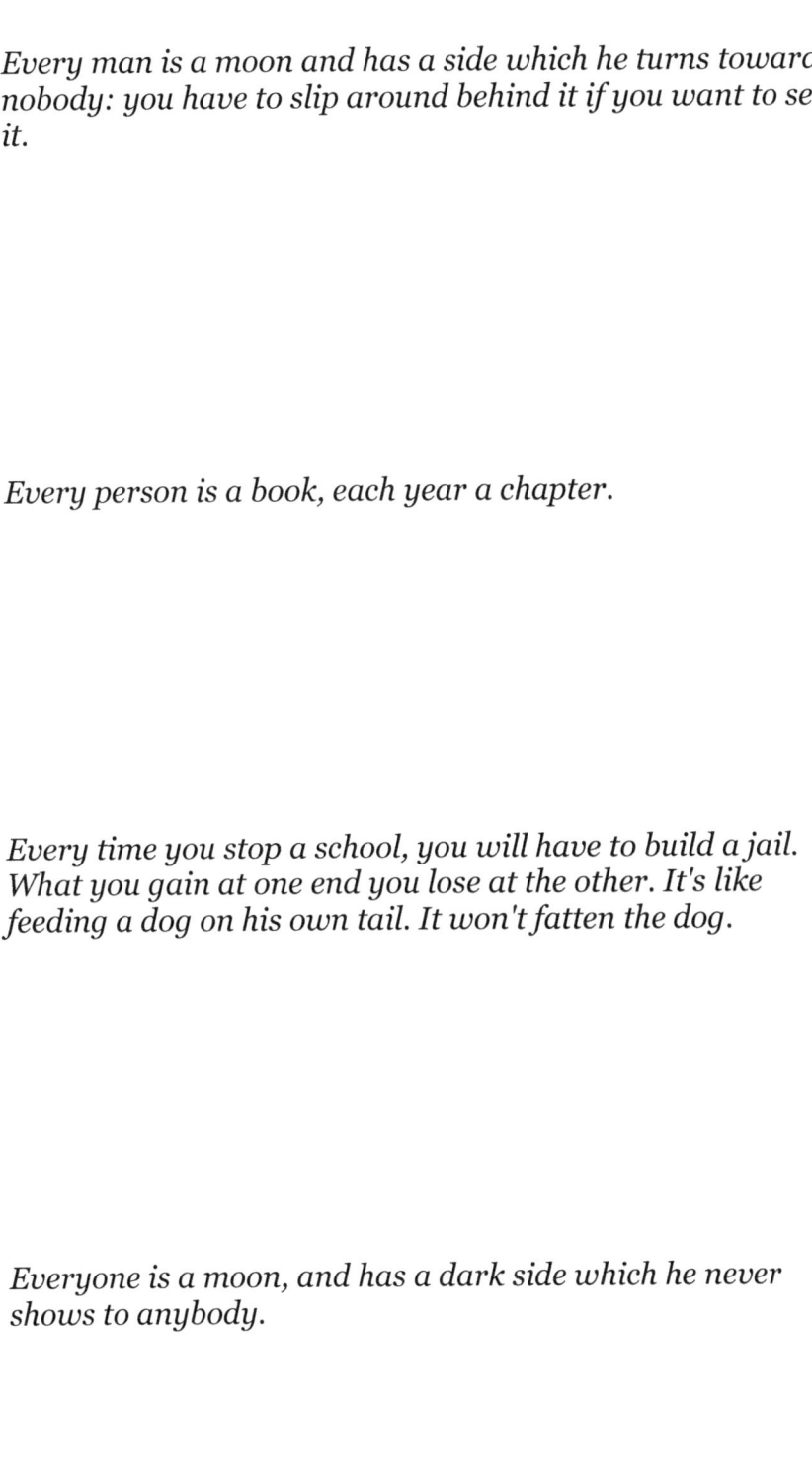

Every man is a moon and has a side which he turns toward nobody: you have to slip around behind it if you want to see it.

Every person is a book, each year a chapter.

Every time you stop a school, you will have to build a jail. What you gain at one end you lose at the other. It's like feeding a dog on his own tail. It won't fatten the dog.

Everyone is a moon, and has a dark side which he never shows to anybody.

Everything has its limit - iron ore cannot be educated into gold.

Everytime I read 'Pride and Prejudice' I want to dig her up and beat her over the skull with her own shin-bone.

Explaining humor is a lot like dissecting a frog, you learn a lot in the process, but in the end you kill it.

Facts are stubborn things, but statistics are pliable.

Fame is a vapor, popularity an accident; the only earthly certainty is oblivion.

Familiarity breeds contempt and children.

Few things are harder to put up with than the annoyance of a good example.

Find a job you enjoy doing, and you will never have to work a day in your life.

Focus more on your desire than on your doubt, and the dream will take care of itself.

For business reasons, I must preserve the outward signs of sanity.

Forgiveness is the fragrance that the violet sheds on the heel that has crushed it.

Get a bicycle. You will not regret it, if you live.

Get your facts first, and then you can distort them as much as you please.

Give a man a reputation as an early riser and he can sleep 'til noon.

Give every day the chance to become the most beautiful day of your life.

Giving up smoking is the easiest thing in the world. I know because I've done it thousands of times.

God created war so that Americans would learn geography.

Good breeding consists of concealing how much we think of ourselves and how little we think of the other person.

Good friends, good books, and a sleepy conscience: this is the ideal life.

Good judgement is the result of experience and experience the result of bad judgement.

Grief can take care of itself, but to get the full value of joy you must have somebody to divide it with.

Habit is habit, and not to be flung out of the window by any man, but coaxed down-stairs one step at a time.

Hain't we got all the fools in town on our side? And hain't that a big enough majority in any town?

Having faith is believing in something you just know ain't true.

He had discovered a great law of human action, without knowing it, namely, that, in order to make a man or a boy covet a thing, it is only necessary to make the thing difficult to attain.

He had had much experience of physicians, and said 'the only way to keep your health is to eat what you don't want, drink what you don't like, and do what you'd druther not'.

He said that man's heart was the only bad heart in the animal kingdom; that man was the only animal capable of feeling malice, envy, vindictiveness, revengefulness, hatred, selfishness, the only animal that loves drunkenness, almost the only animal that could endure personal uncleanliness and a filthy habitation, the sole animal in whom was fully developed the base instinct called patriotism, the sole animal that robs, persecutes, oppresses and kills members of his own tribe, the sole animal that steals and enslaves the members of any tribe.

He was sunshine most always-I mean he made it seem like good weather.

He who asks is a fool for five minutes, but he who does not ask remains a fool forever.

Heaven goes by favor. If it went by merit, you would stay out and your dog would go in.

Herodotus says, Very few things happen at the right time, and the rest do not happen at all: the conscientious historian will correct these defects.

High and fine literature is wine, and mine is only water; but everybody likes water.

His head was an hour-glass; it could stow an idea, but it had to do it a grain at a time, not the whole idea at once.

History doesn't repeat itself, but it does rhyme.

Honesty: The best of all the lost arts.

How little a thing can make us happy when we feel that we have earned it.

How often we recall with regret that Napoleon once shot at a magazine editor and missed him and killed a publisher. But we remember with charity that his intentions were good.

Huck was always willing to take a hand in any enterprise that offered entertainment and required no capital, for he had a troublesome super-abundance of that sort of time which is not money.

Human beings can be awful cruel to one another.

Human pride is not worthwhile; there is always something lying in wait to take the wind out of it.

Humor is mankind's greatest blessing.

Humor is the great thing, the saving thing. The minute it crops up, all our irritations and resentments slip away and a sunny spirit takes their place.

Humor is tragedy plus time.

I always take Scotch whiskey at night as a preventive of toothache. I have never had the toothache; and what is more, I never intend to have it.

I am a great and sublime fool. But then I am God's fool, and all His works must be contemplated with respect.

I am an old man and have known a great many troubles, but most of them have never happened.

I am not one of those who in expressing opinions confine themselves to facts.

I apologize for such a long letter - I didn't have time to write a short one.

I can last two months on a good compliment.

I can teach anybody how to get what they want out of life. The problem is that I can't find anybody who can tell me what they want.

I cannot call to mind a single instance where I have ever been irreverent, except toward the things which were sacred to other people.

I couldn't bear to think about it; and yet, somehow, I couldn't think about nothing else.

I did not attend his funeral, but I sent a nice letter saying I approved of it.

I didn't have time to write a short letter, so I wrote a long one instead.

I do not fear death. I had been dead for billions and billions of years before I was born, and had not suffered the slightest inconvenience from it.

I do not like work even when someone else is doing it.

I do not wish any reward but to know I have done the right thing.

I don't like to commit myself about Heaven and Hell, you see, I have friends in both places.

I don't see any use in having a uniform and arbitrary way of spelling words. We might as well make all clothes alike and cook all dishes alike. Sameness is tiresome; variety is pleasing.

I don't want no better book than what your face is.

I felt so lonesome I most wished I was dead. The stars were shining, and the leaves rustled in the woods ever so mournful; and I heard an owl, away off, who-whooing about somebody that was dead, and a whippowill and a dog crying about somebody that was going to die.

I have a higher and grander standard of principle than George Washington. He could not lie; I can, but I won't.

I have been complimented many times and they always embarrass me; I always feel they have not said enough.

I have been studying the traits and dispositions of the lower animals (so called) and contrasting them with the traits and dispositions of man. I find the result humiliating to me.

I have found out that there ain't no surer way to find out whether you like people or hate them than to travel with them.

I have never let my schooling interfere with my education.

I haven't any right to criticize books, and I don't do it except when I hate them. I often want to criticize Jane Austen, but her books madden me so that I can't conceal my frenzy from the reader; and therefore I have to stop every time I begin.

I know the look of an apple that is roasting and sizzling on the hearth on a winter's evening, and I know the comfort that comes of eating it hot, along with some sugar and a drench of cream... I know how the nuts taken in conjunction with winter apples, cider, and doughnuts, make old people's tales and old jokes sound fresh and crisp and enchanting.

I know your race. It is made up of sheep. It is governed by minorities, seldom or never by majorities. It suppresses its feelings and its beliefs and follows the handful that makes the most noise. Sometimes the noisy handful is right, sometimes wrong; but no matter, the crowd follows it. The vast majority of the race, whether savage or civilized, are secretly kind-hearted and shrink from inflicting pain, but in the presence of the aggressive and pitiless minority they don't dare to assert themselves. Think of it! One kind-hearted creature spies upon another, and sees to it that he loyally helps in iniquities which revolt both of them. Speaking as an expert, I know that ninety- nine out of a hundred of your race were strongly against the killing of witches when that foolishness was first agitated by a handful of pious lunatics in the long ago. And I know that even to-day, after ages of transmitted prejudice and silly teaching, only one person in twenty puts any real heart into the harrying of a witch. And yet apparently everybody hates witches and wants them killed. Some day a handful will rise up on the other side and make the most noise--perhaps even a single daring man with a big voice and a determined front will do it--and in a week all the sheep will wheel and follow him, and witch-hunting will come to a sudden end.

Monarchies, aristocracies, and religions are all based upon that large defect in your race--the individual's distrust of his neighbor, and his desire, for safety's or comfort's sake, to stand well in his neighbor's eye. These institutions will always remain, and always flourish, and always oppress you, affront you, and degrade you, because you will always be and remain slaves of minorities. There was never a country where the majority of the people were in their secret hearts loyal to any of these institutions.

I must have a prodigious amount of mind; it takes me as much as a week, sometimes, to make it up!

I notice that you use plain, simple language, short words and brief sentences. That is the way to write English—it is the modern way and the best way. Stick to it; don't let fluff and flowers and verbosity creep in. When you catch an adjective, kill it. No, I don't mean utterly, but kill most of them—then the rest will be valuable. They weaken when they are close together. They give strength when they are wide apart. An adjective habit, or a wordy, diffuse, flowery habit, once fastened upon a person, is as hard to get rid of as any other vice.

I once sent a dozen of my friends a telegram saying 'flee at once - all is discovered.' They all left town immediately.

I said there was nothing so convincing to an Indian as a general massacre. If he could not approve of the massacre, I said the next surest thing for an Indian was soap and education. Soap and education are not as sudden as a massacre, but they are more deadly in the long run; because a half-massacred Indian may recover, but if you educate him and wash him, it is bound to finish him some time or other.

I take my only exercise acting as a pallbearer at the funerals of my friends who exercise regularly.

I think that to one in sympathy with nature, each season, in turn, seems the loveliest.

I thoroughly disapprove of duels. If a man should challenge me, I would take him kindly and forgivingly by the hand and lead him to a quiet place and kill him.

I was born lazy. I am no lazier now than I was forty years ago, but that is because I reached the limit forty years ago. You can't go beyond possibility.

I was gratified to be able to answer promptly, and I did. I said I didn't know.

I was sorry to have my name mentioned as one of the great authors, because they have a sad habit of dying off. Chaucer is dead, Spencer is dead, so is Milton, so is Shakespeare, and I'm not feeling so well myself.

I wish I could make him understand that a loving good heart is riches enough, and that without it intellect is poverty.

I wonder if God created man because He was disappointed with the monkey.

I've had a lot of worries in my life, most of which never happened.

I've lived through some terrible things in my life, some of which actually happened.

If a person offends you, and you are in doubt as to whether it was intentional or not, do not resort to extreme measures; simply watch your chance, and hit him with a brick.

If animals could speak, the dog would be a blundering outspoken fellow; but the cat would have the rare grace of never saying a word too much.

If books are not good company, where shall I find it?

If Christ were here there is one thing he would not be—a Christian.

If everyone was satisfied with himself, there would be no heroes.

If man could be crossed with a cat, it would improve man but deteriorate the cat.

If people are good only because they fear punishment, and hope for reward, then we are a sorry lot indeed.

If voting made any difference they wouldn't let us do it.

If we would learn what the human race really is at bottom, we need only observe it in election times.

If you don't read the newspaper, you're uninformed. If you read the newspaper, you're mis-informed.

If you must be indiscrete, be discrete in your indiscretion.

If you pick up a starving dog and make him prosperous he will not bite you. This is the principal difference between a dog and man.

If you tell the truth you do not need a good memory!

If you tell the truth, you don't have to remember anything.

If you want me to give you a two-hour presentation, I am ready today. If you want only a five-minute speech, it will take me two weeks to prepare.

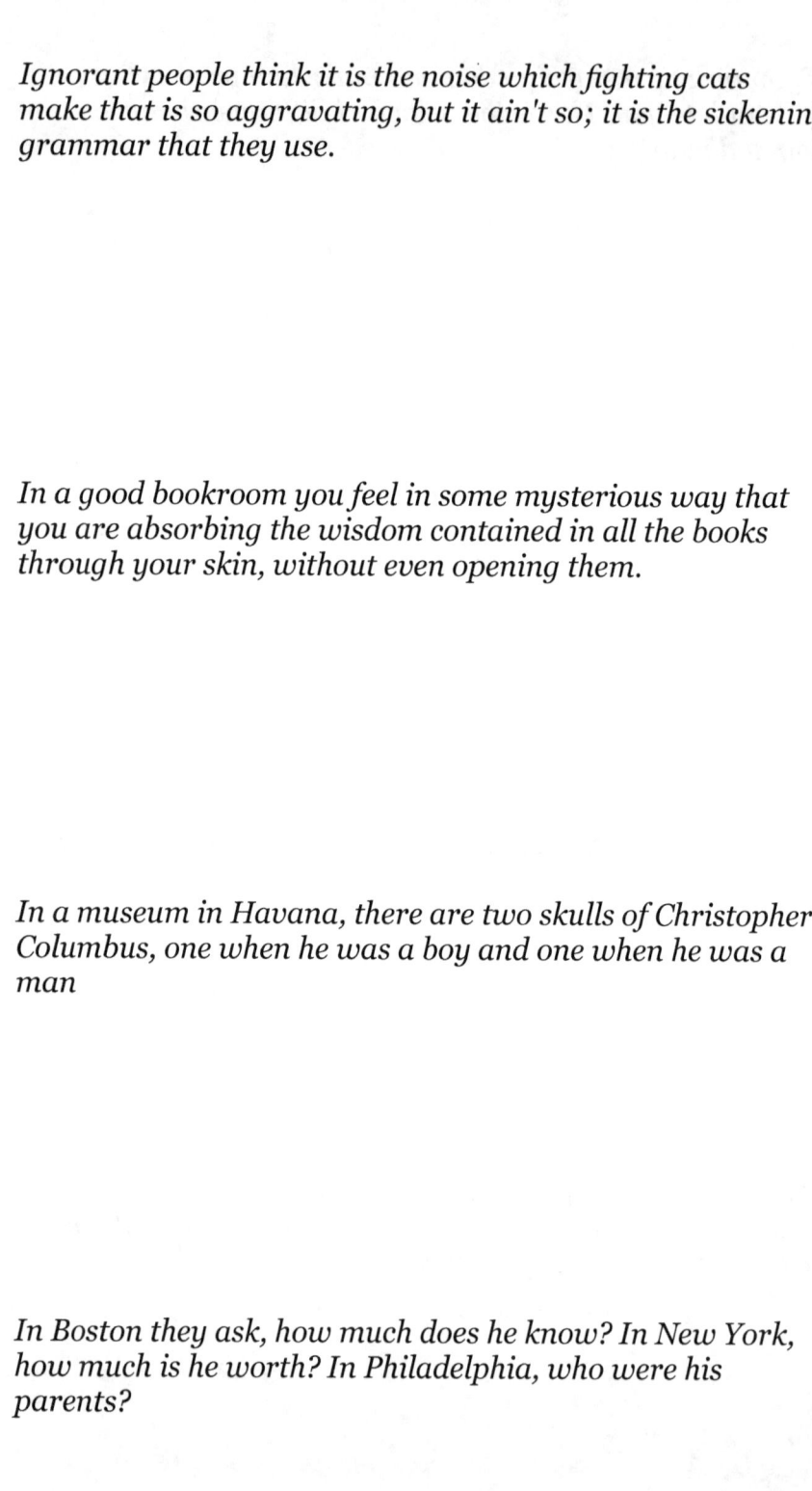

Ignorant people think it is the noise which fighting cats make that is so aggravating, but it ain't so; it is the sickening grammar that they use.

In a good bookroom you feel in some mysterious way that you are absorbing the wisdom contained in all the books through your skin, without even opening them.

In a museum in Havana, there are two skulls of Christopher Columbus, one when he was a boy and one when he was a man

In Boston they ask, how much does he know? In New York, how much is he worth? In Philadelphia, who were his parents?

In Paris they just simply opened their eyes and stared when we spoke to them in French! We never did succeed in making those idiots understand their own language.

In religion and politics people's beliefs and convictions are in almost every case gotten at second-hand, and without examination, from authorities who have not themselves examined the questions at issue but have taken them at second-hand from other non-examiners, whose opinions about them were not worth a brass farthing.

In the beginning of a change the patriot is a scarce man, and brave, and hated and scorned. When his cause succeeds, the timid join him, for then it costs nothing to be a patriot.

In the first place God made idiots. This was for practice. Then he made school boards.

It ain't the parts of the Bible that I can't understand that bother me, it's the parts that I do understand.

It ain't what you don't know that gets you into trouble. It's what you know for sure that just ain't so.

It could probably be shown by facts and figures that there is no distinctly native American criminal class except Congress.

It is better to be alone than unwelcome. - Eve

It is better to deserve honors and not have them than to have them and not deserve them.

It is by the goodness of God that in our country we have those three unspeakably precious things: freedom of speech, freedom of conscience, and the prudence never to practice either of them.

It is curious that physical courage should be so common in the world and moral courage so rare.

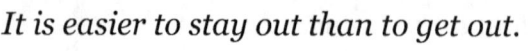

It is easier to stay out than to get out.

It is higher and nobler to be kind.

It is just like man's vanity and impertinence to call an animal dumb because it is dumb to his dull perceptions. Heaven is by favor; if it were by merit your dog would go in and you would stay out. Of all the creatures ever made he (man) is the most detestable. Of the entire brood, he is the only one...that possesses malice. He is the only creature that inflicts pain for sport, knowing it to be pain. The fact that man knows right from wrong proves his intellectual superiority to the other creatures; but the fact that he can do wrong proves his moral inferiority to any creature that cannot.

It is sound judgment to put on a bold face and play your hand for a hundred times what it is worth; forty-nine times out of fifty nobody dares to call it, and you roll in the chips.

It is true, that which I have revealed to you; there is no God, no universe, no human race, no earthly life, no heaven, no hell. It is all a dream--a grotesque and foolish dream. Nothing exists but you. And you are but a thought--a vagrant thought, a useless thought, a homeless thought, wandering forlorn among the empty eternities!

It made me shiver. And I about made up my mind to pray, and see if I couldn't try to quit being the kind of a boy I was and be better. So I kneeled down. But the words wouldn't come. Why wouldn't they? It warn't no use to try and hide it from Him. Nor from ME, neither. I knowed very well why they wouldn't come. It was because my heart warn't right; it was because I warn't square; it was because I was playing double. I was letting ON to give up sin, but away inside of me I was holding on to the biggest one of all. I was trying to make my mouth SAY I would do the right thing and the clean thing, and go and write to that nigger's owner and tell where he was; but deep down in me I knowed it was a lie, and He knowed it. You can't pray a lie--I found that out.

So I was full of trouble, full as I could be; and didn't know what to do. At last I had an idea; and I says, I'll go and write the letter--and then see if I can pray. Why, it was astonishing, the way I felt as light as a feather right straight off, and my troubles all gone. So I got a piece of paper and a pencil, all glad and excited, and set down and wrote:

Miss Watson, your runaway nigger Jim is down here two mile below Pikesville, and Mr. Phelps has got him and he will give him up for the reward if you send.

HUCK FINN.

I felt good and all washed clean of sin for the first time I had ever felt so in my life, and I knowed I could pray now. But I didn't do it straight off, but laid the paper down and set there thinking--thinking how good it was all this happened so, and how near I come to being lost and going to hell. And went on thinking. And got to thinking over our trip down the river; and I see Jim before me all the time: in the day and in the night-time, sometimes moonlight, sometimes storms, and we a-floating along, talking and singing and laughing. But somehow I couldn't seem to strike no places to harden me against him, but only the other kind. I'd see him standing my watch on top of his'n, 'stead of calling me, so I could go on sleeping; and see him how glad he was when I come back out of the fog; and when I come to him again in the swamp, up there where the feud was; and such-like times; and would always call me honey, and pet me and do everything he could think of for me, and how good he always was; and at last I struck the time I saved him by telling the men we had small-pox aboard, and he was so grateful, and said I was the best friend old Jim ever had in the world, and the ONLY one he's got now; and then I happened to look around and see that paper.

It was a close place. I took it up, and held it in my hand. I was a-trembling, because I'd got to decide, forever, betwixt two things, and I knowed it. I studied a minute, sort of *holding my breath, and then says to myself:*

All right, then, I'll GO to hell--and tore it up.

It may have happened, it may not have happened, but it could have happened.

It takes your enemy and your friend, working together, to hurt you to the heart: the one to slander you and the other to get the news to you.

It usually takes me two or three days to prepare an impromptu speech.

It's better to keep your mouth shut and appear stupid than open it and remove all doubt

It's easier to fool people than to convince them that they have been fooled.

It's easy to make friends, but hard to get rid of them.

It's lovely to live on a raft. We had the sky, up there, all speckled with stars, and we used to lay on our backs and look up at them, and discuss about whether they was made, or only just happened- Jim he allowed they was made, but I allowed they happened; I judged it would have took too long to make so many.

It's not as bad as it sounds.

It's not the good that die young, it's the lucky.

Jim said that bees won't sting idiots, but I didn't believe that, because I tried them lots of times myself and they wouldn't sting me.

Just the omission of Jane Austen's books alone would make a fairly good library out of a library that hadn't a book in it.

Just when I thought I was learning how to live, 'twas then I realized I was learning how to die.

Keep away from people who try to belittle your ambitions. Small people always do that but the really great make you feel that you too can become great. When you are seeking to bring big plans to fruition it is important with whom you regularly associate. Hang out with friends who are like-minded and who are also designing purpose-filled lives. Similarly be that kind of a friend for your friends.

Kindness is a language which the deaf can hear and the blind can see.

Learning softeneth the heart and breedeth gentleness and charity.

Let us be thankful for the fools. But for them the rest of us could not succeed.

Let us consider that we are all partially insane. It will explain us to each other; it will unriddle many riddles; it will make clear and simple many things which are involved in haunting and harassing difficulties and obscurities now.

Let us draw the curtain of charity over the rest of this scene

Let us endeavor so to live that when we come to die even the undertaker will be sorry.

Let us live so that when we come to die even the undertaker will be sorry.

Let us make a special effort to stop communicating with each other, so we can have some conversation.

Let us not be too particular. It is better to have old second-hand diamonds than none at all.

Life does not consist mainly, or even largely, of facts or happenings. It consist mainly of the storm of thoughts that is forever flowing through one's head.

Love is not a product of reasonings and statistics. It just comes-none knows whence-and cannot explain itself.

Love seems the swiftest, but it is the slowest of all growths. No man or woman really knows what perfect love is until they have been married a quarter of a century.

Loyalty to a petrified opinion never yet broke a chain or freed a human soul.

Loyalty to country ALWAYS. Loyalty to government, when it deserves it.

Man - a figment of God's imagination.

Man has imagined a heaven, and has left entirely out of it the supremest of all his delights...sexual intercourse!...His heaven is like himself: strange, interesting, astonishing, grotesque. I give you my word, it has not a single feature in it that he actually values.

Man is a Religious Animal. He is the only Religious Animal. He is the only animal that has the True Religion--several of them. He is the only animal that loves his neighbor as himself and cuts his throat if his theology isn't straight. He has made a graveyard of the globe in trying his honest best to smooth his brother's path to happiness and heaven....The higher animals have no religion. And we are told that they are going to be left out in the Hereafter. I wonder why? It seems questionable taste.

Man is the only animal that blushes. Or needs to.

Man is the only animal that deals in that atrocity of atrocities War. He is the only one that gathers his brethren about him and goes forth in cold blood and calm pulse to exterminate his kind. He is the only animal that for sordid wages will march out... and help to slaughter strangers of his own species who have done him no harm and with whom he has no quarrel.... And in the intervals between campaigns he washes the blood off his hands and works for the universal brotherhood of man with his mouth.

Man is the Reasoning Animal. Such is the claim. I think it is open to dispute. Indeed, my experiments have proven to me that he is the Unreasoning Animal... In truth, man is incurably foolish. Simple things which other animals easily learn, he is incapable of learning. Among my experiments was this. In an hour I taught a cat and a dog to be friends. I put them in a cage. In another hour I taught them to be friends with a rabbit. In the course of two days I was able to add a fox, a goose, a squirrel and some doves. Finally a monkey. They lived together in peace; even affectionately.

Next, in another cage I confined an Irish Catholic from Tipperary, and as soon as he seemed tame I added a Scotch Presbyterian from Aberdeen. Next a Turk from Constantinople; a Greek Christian from Crete; an Armenian; a Methodist from the wilds of Arkansas; a Buddhist from China; a Brahman from Benares. Finally, a Salvation Army Colonel from Wapping. Then I stayed away for two whole days. When I came back to note results, the cage of Higher Animals was all right, but in the other there was but a chaos of gory odds and ends of turbans and fezzes and plaids and bones and flesh--not a specimen left alive. These Reasoning Animals had disagreed on a theological detail and carried the matter to a Higher Court.

Man was made at the end of the week's work when God was tired.

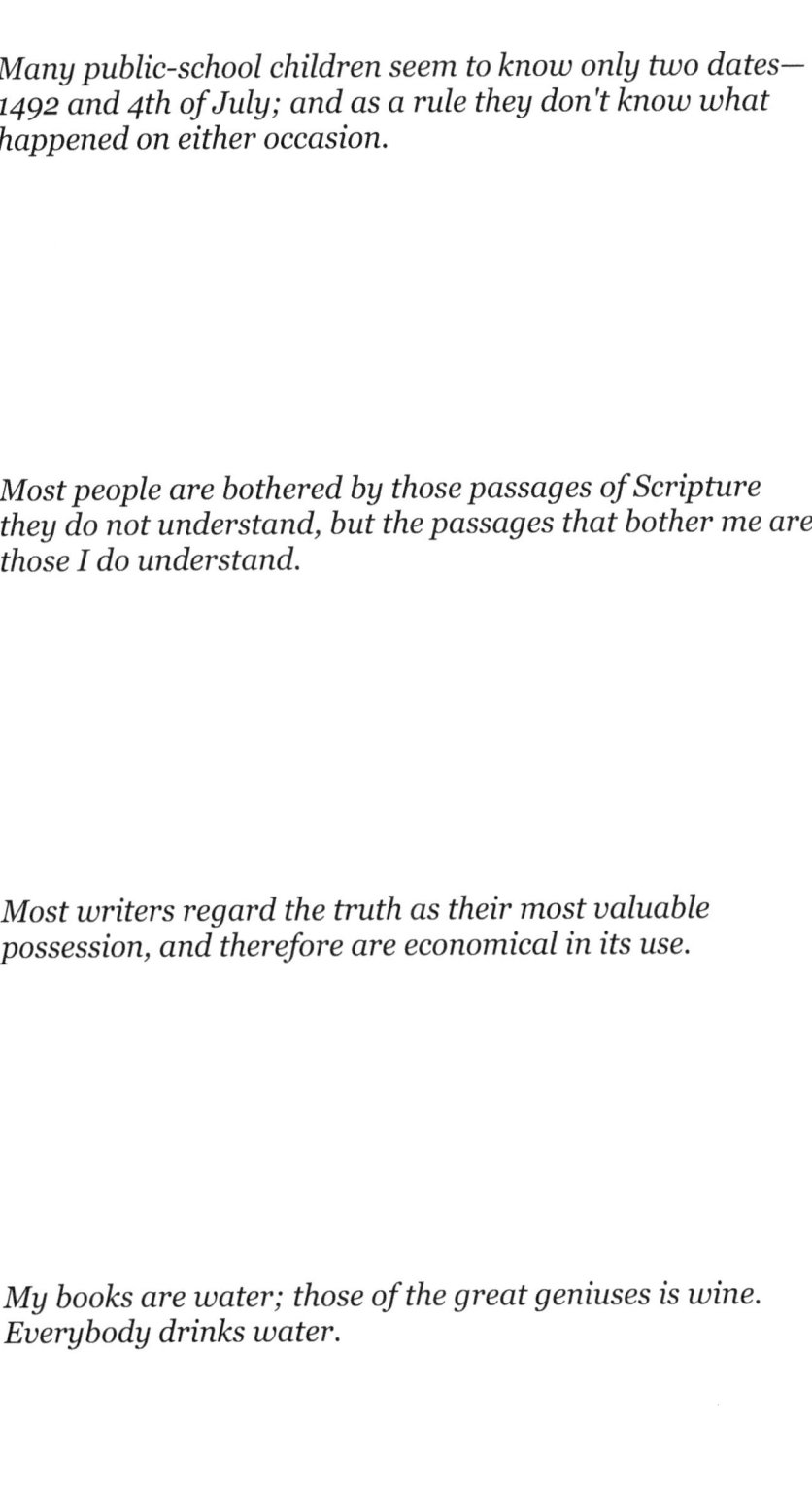

Many public-school children seem to know only two dates—1492 and 4th of July; and as a rule they don't know what happened on either occasion.

Most people are bothered by those passages of Scripture they do not understand, but the passages that bother me are those I do understand.

Most writers regard the truth as their most valuable possession, and therefore are economical in its use.

My books are water; those of the great geniuses is wine. Everybody drinks water.

My kind of loyalty was loyalty to one's country, not to its institutions or its officeholders. The country is the real thing, the substantial thing, the eternal thing; it is the thing to watch over, and care for, and be loyal to; institutions are extraneous, they are its mere clothing, and clothing can wear out, become ragged, cease to be comfortable, cease to protect the body from winter, disease, and death.

Name the greatest of all inventors. Accident.

Nature knows no indecencies; man invents them.

Necessity is the mother of taking chances.

Never allow someone to be your priority while allowing yourself to be their option.

Never argue with a fool, onlookers may not be able to tell the difference.

Never argue with an idiot. They will drag you down to their level and beat you with experience.

Never be haughty to the humble, never be humble to the haughty.

Never have a battle of wits with an unarmed person.

Never let the truth get in the way of a good story.

Never put off till tomorrow what may be done day after tomorrow just as well.

Never tell the truth to people who are not worthy of it.

New Orleans food is as delicious as the less criminal forms of sin.

New Year's Day: Now is the accepted time to make your regular annual good resolutions. Next week you can begin paving hell with them as usual.

Noise proves nothing. Often a hen who has laid an egg cackles as if she had laid an asteroid.

Nothing exists but you. And you are but a thought.

Nothing exists; all is a dream. God—man—the world—the sun, the moon, the wilderness of stars—a dream, all a dream; they have no existence. Nothing exists save empty space—and you!

Nothing so needs reforming as other people's habits.

Nothing that grieves us can be called little: by the eternal laws of proportion a child's loss of a doll and a king's loss of a crown are events of the same size.

Now and then we had a hope that if we lived and were good, God would permit us to be pirates.

Now he found out a new thing--namely, that to promise not to do a thing is the surest way in the world to make a body want to go and do that very thing.

Obscurity and a competence—that is the life that is best worth living.

October: This is one of the peculiarly dangerous months to speculate in stocks. The others are July, January, September, April, November, May, March, June, December, August and February.

Of all God's creatures, there is only one that cannot be made slave of the leash. That one is the cat. If man could be crossed with the cat it would improve the man, but it would deteriorate the cat.

Of all the animals, man is the only one that is cruel. He is the only one that inflicts pain for the pleasure of doing it.

Often it does seem such a pity that Noah and his party did not miss the boat.

One frequently only finds out how really beautiful a women is, until after considerable acquaintance with her.

One must travel, to learn. Every day, now, old Scriptural phrases that never possessed any significance for me before, take to themselves a meaning.

One of the most striking differences between a cat and a lie is that a cat has only nine lives.

One should never use exclamation points in writing. It is like laughing at your own joke.

Only one thing is impossible for God: To find any sense in any copyright law on the planet.

Out of all the things I have lost, I miss my mind the most.

Part of the secret of success in life is to eat what you like and let the food fight it out inside.

Patriotism is supporting your country all the time and your government when it deserves it.

Peace by persuasion has a pleasant sound, but I think we should not be able to work it. We should have to tame the human race first, and history seems to show that that cannot be done.

People talk about beautiful relationships between two persons of the same sex. What is the best of that sort as compared with the friendship of man and wife where the best impulses and highest ideals of both are the same? There is no place for comparison between the two friendships; the one is earthly, the other divine.

Persons attempting to find a motive in this narrative will be prosecuted; persons attempting to find a moral in it will be banished; persons attempting to find a plot in it will be shot.

Plain question and plain answer make the shortest road out of most perplexities.

Politicians and diapers must be changed often, and for the same reason.

Reader, suppose you were an idiot. And suppose you were a member of Congress. But I repeat myself.

Reality can be beaten with enough imagination.

Really great people make you feel that you, too, can become great.

Religion was invented when the first con man met the first fool.

Right is right, and wrong is wrong, and a body ain't got no business doing wrong when he ain't ignorant and knows better.

Sanity and happiness are an impossible combination.

Satan hasn't a single salaried helper; the Opposition employs a million.

Saturday morning was come, and all the summer world was bright and fresh, and brimming with life. There was a song in every heart; and if the heart was young, the music issued at the lips. There was cheer in every face and a spring in every step. The locust-trees were in bloom, and the fragrance of the blossoms filled the air. Cardiff Hill, beyond the village and above, it was green with vegetation, and it lay just far enough away to seem a Delectable Land, dreamy, reposeful, and inviting.

She remained both girl and woman to the last day of her life. Under a grave and gentle exterior burned inextinguishable fires of sympathy, energy, devotion, enthusiasm, and absolutely limitless affection.

She was not quite what you would call refined. She was not quite what you would call unrefined. She was the kind of person that keeps a parrot.

Some people get an education without going to college. The rest get it after they get out.

Sometimes you gwyne to git hurt, en sometimes you gwyne to git sick; but every time you's gwyne to git well agin.

Stars and shadows ain't good to see by.

Strange! that you should not have suspected years ago--centuries, ages, eons, ago!--for you have existed, companionless, through all the eternities. Strange, indeed, that you should not have suspected that your universe and its contents were only dreams, visions, fiction! Strange, because they are so frankly and hysterically insane--like all dreams: a God who could make good children as easily as bad, yet preferred to make bad ones; who could have made every one of them happy, yet never made a single happy one; who made them prize their bitter life, yet stingily cut it short; who gave his angels eternal happiness unearned, yet required his other children to earn it; who gave his angels painless lives, yet cursed his other children with biting miseries and maladies of mind and body; who mouths justice and invented hell--mouths mercy and invented hell--mouths Golden Rules, and forgiveness multiplied by seventy times seven, and invented hell; who mouths morals to other people and has none himself; who frowns upon crimes, yet commits them all; who created man without invitation, then tries to shuffle the responsibility for man's acts upon man, instead of honorably placing it where it belongs, upon himself; and finally, with altogether divine obtuseness, invites this poor, abused slave to worship him!

Substitute 'damn' every time you're inclined to write 'very;' your editor will delete it and the writing will be just as it should be.

Thanksgiving Day, a function which originated in New England two or three centuries ago when those people recognized that they really had something to be thankful for -- annually, not oftener -- if they had succeeded in exterminating their neighbors, the Indians, during the previous twelve months instead of getting exterminated by their neighbors, the Indians. Thanksgiving Day became a habit, for the reason that in the course of time, as the years drifted on, it was perceived that the exterminating had ceased to be mutual and was all on the white man's side, consequently on the Lord's side; hence it was proper to thank the Lord for it and extend the usual annual compliments.

That is just the way with some people. They get down on a thing when they don't know nothing about it.

That's the difference between governments and individuals. Governments don't care, individuals do.

The average man don't like trouble and danger.

The best way to cheer yourself is to try to cheer someone else up.

The Bible has noble poetry in it... and some good morals and a wealth of obscenity, and upwards of a thousand lies.

The coldest winter I ever spent was a summer in San Francisco.

The common eye sees only the outside of things, and judges by that, but the seeing eye pierces through and reads the heart and the soul, finding there capacities which the outside didn't indicate or promise, and which the other kind of eye couldn't detect.

The difference between a Miracle and a Fact is exactly the difference between a mermaid and a seal.

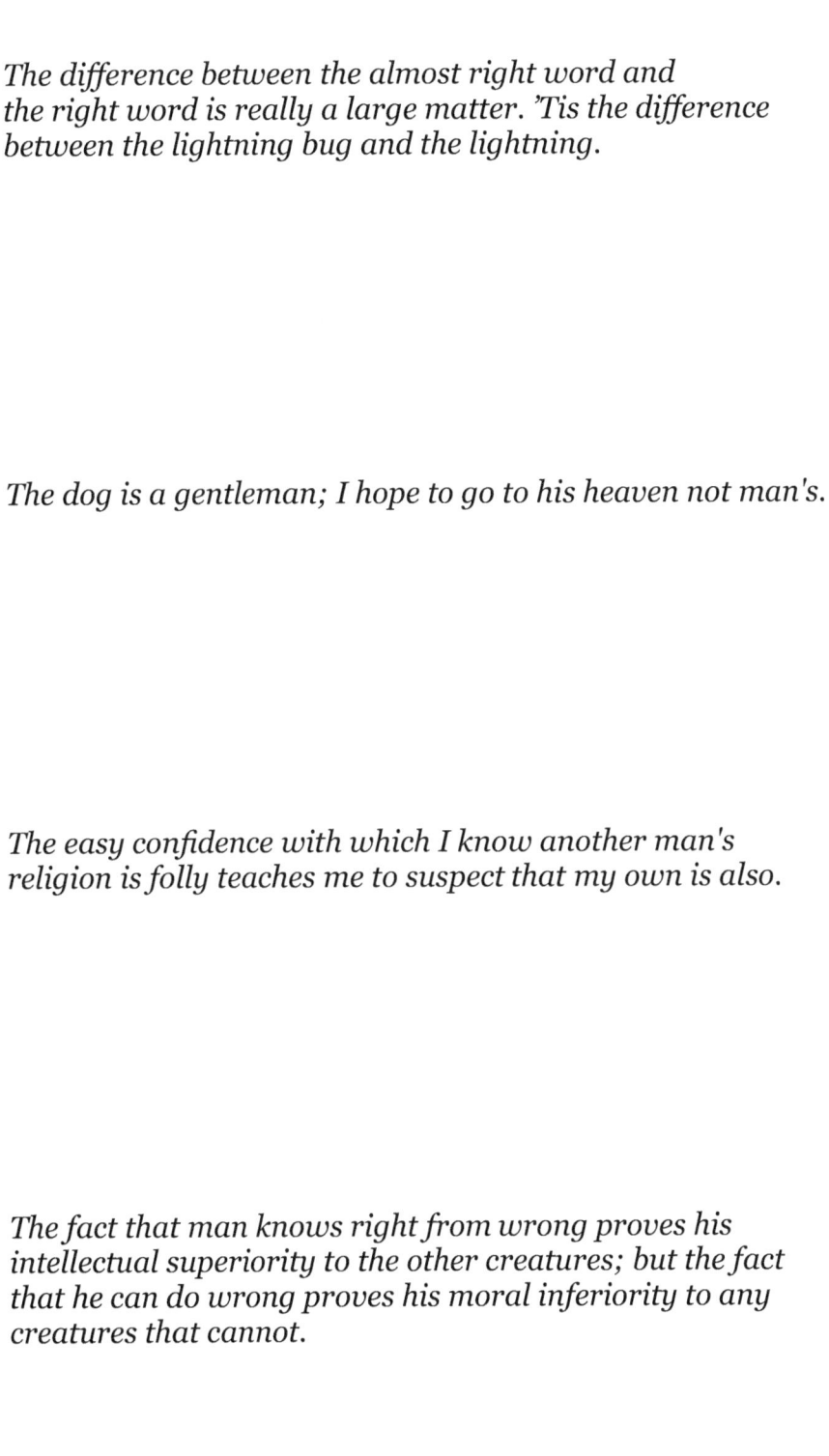

The difference between the almost right word and the right word is really a large matter. 'Tis the difference between the lightning bug and the lightning.

The dog is a gentleman; I hope to go to his heaven not man's.

The easy confidence with which I know another man's religion is folly teaches me to suspect that my own is also.

The fact that man knows right from wrong proves his intellectual superiority to the other creatures; but the fact that he can do wrong proves his moral inferiority to any creatures that cannot.

The fear of death follows from the fear of life. A man who lives fully is prepared to die at any time.

The gentle reader will never, never know what a consummate ass he can become until he goes abroad. I speak now, of course, in the supposition that the gentle reader has not been abroad, and therefore is not already a consummate ass. If the case be otherwise, I beg his pardon and extend to him the cordial hand of fellowship and call him brother. I shall always delight to meet an ass after my own heart when I have finished my travels.

The government is merely a servant—merely a temporary servant; it cannot be its prerogative to determine what is right and what is wrong, and decide who is a patriot and who isn't. Its function is to obey orders, not originate them.

The holy passion of Friendship is of so sweet and steady and loyal and enduring a nature that it will last through a whole lifetime, if not asked to lend money.

The human race has only one really effective weapon and that is laughter.

The lack of money is the root of all evil.

The less there is to justify a traditional custom, the harder it is to get rid of it

The man who does not read has no advantage over the man who cannot read.

The man who is a pessimist before 48 knows too much; if he is an optimist after it he knows too little.

The more I learn about people, the more I like my dog.

The more things are forbidden, the more popular they become.

The most interesting information come from children, for they tell all they know and then stop.

The older I get, the more clearly I remember things that never happened.

The only difference between a tax man and a taxidermist is that the taxidermist leaves the skin.

The only difference between reality and fiction is that fiction needs to be credible.

The pitifulest thing out is a mob; that's what an army is--a mob; they don't fight with courage that's born in them, but with courage that's borrowed from their mass, and from their officers. But a mob without any MAN at the head of it is BENEATH pitifulness.

The proper office of a friend is to side with you when you are in the wrong. Nearly anybody will side with you when you are in the right.

The radical of one century is the conservative of the next. The radical invents the views. When he has worn them out, the conservative adopt.

The reports of my death are greatly exaggerated.

The right word may be effective, but no word was ever as effective as a rightly timed pause.

The rule is perfect: in all matters of opinion our adversaries are insane.

The secret of getting ahead is getting started. The secret of getting started is breaking your complex overwhelming tasks into small manageable tasks, and starting on the first one.

The secret source of humor is not joy but sorrow; there is no humor in heaven.

The secret to getting ahead is getting started.

The so-called Christian nations are the most enlightened and progressive ... but in spite of their religion, not because of it. The Church has opposed every innovation and discovery from the day of Galileo down to our own time, when the use of anesthetic in childbirth was regarded as a sin because it avoided the biblical curse pronounced against Eve. And every step in astronomy and geology ever taken has been opposed by bigotry and superstition. The Greeks surpassed us in artistic culture and in architecture five hundred years before Christian religion was born.

The source of all humor is not laughter, but sorrow.

The test of any good fiction is that you should care something for the characters; the good to succeed, the bad to fail. The trouble with most fiction is that you want them all to land in hell together, as quickly as possible.

The trouble ain't that there is too many fools, but that the lightning ain't distributed right.

The trouble is not in dying for a friend, but in finding a friend worth dying for.

The trouble with the world is not that people know too little; it's that they know so many things that just aren't so.

The two most important days in your life are the day you are born and the day you find out why.

The very ink with which all history is written is merely fluid prejudice.

The worst loneliness is to not be comfortable with yourself.

There are many humorous things in the world; among them, the white man's notion that he is less savage than the other savages.

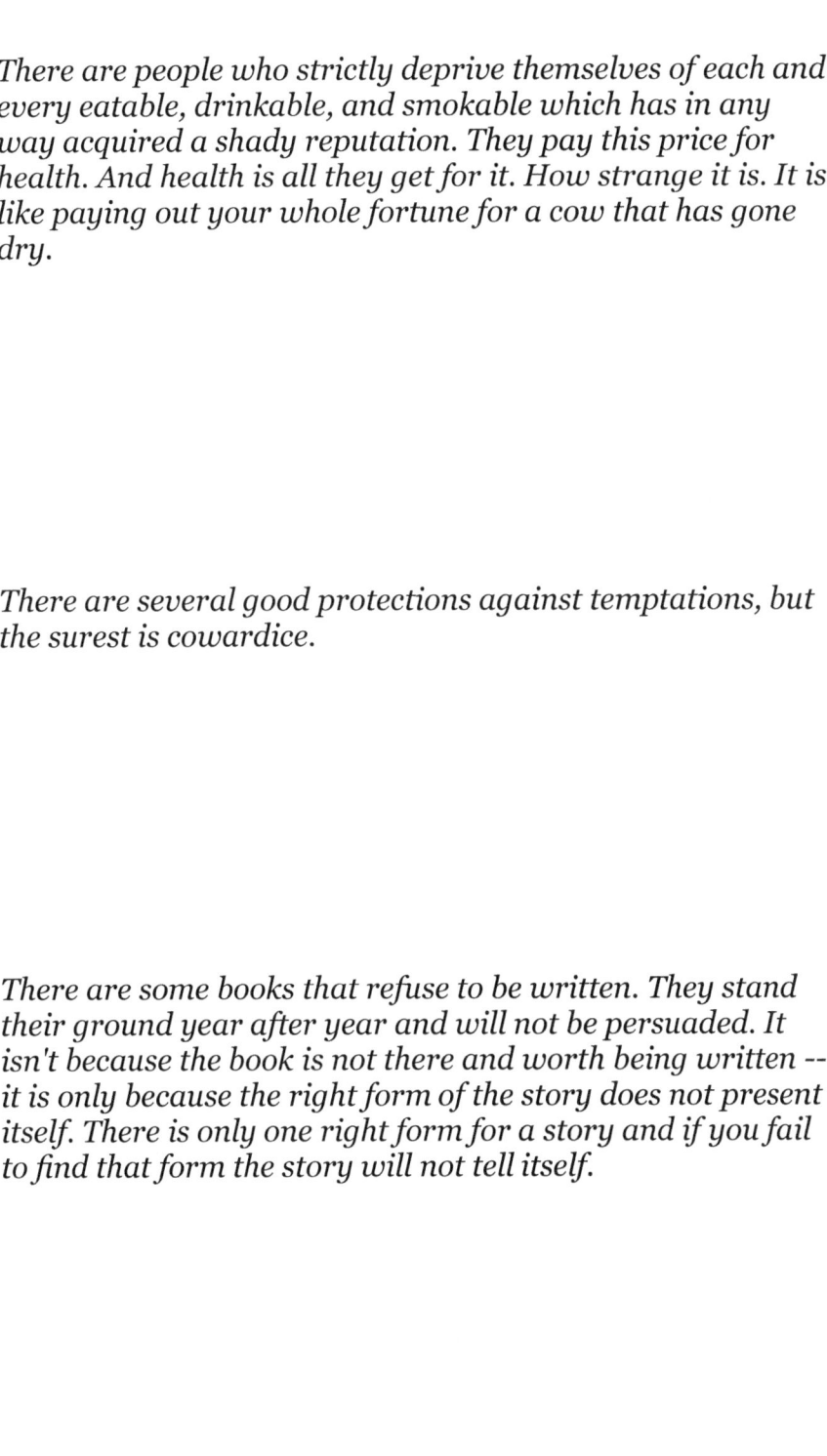

There are people who strictly deprive themselves of each and every eatable, drinkable, and smokable which has in any way acquired a shady reputation. They pay this price for health. And health is all they get for it. How strange it is. It is like paying out your whole fortune for a cow that has gone dry.

There are several good protections against temptations, but the surest is cowardice.

There are some books that refuse to be written. They stand their ground year after year and will not be persuaded. It isn't because the book is not there and worth being written -- it is only because the right form of the story does not present itself. There is only one right form for a story and if you fail to find that form the story will not tell itself.

There are some few people I respect and admire, but I don't think much of the species.

There are those who scoff at the schoolboy, calling him frivolous and shallow: Yet it was the schoolboy who said 'Faith is believing what you know ain't so'.

There are three things men can do with women: love them, suffer them, or turn them into literature.

There are two kinds of patriotism -- monarchical patriotism and republican patriotism. In the one case the government and the king may rightfully furnish you their notions of patriotism; in the other, neither the government nor the entire nation is privileged to dictate to any individual what the form of his patriotism shall be. The gospel of the monarchical patriotism is: The King can do no wrong. We have adopted it with all its servility, with an unimportant change in the wording: Our country, right or wrong! We have thrown away the most valuable asset we had:-- the individual's right to oppose both flag and country when he (just he, by himself) believed them to be in the wrong. We have thrown it away; and with it all that was really respectable about that grotesque and laughable word, Patriotism.

There has never been a just [war], never an honorable one-- on the part of the instigator of the war. I can see a million years ahead, and this rule will never change in so many as half a dozen instances. The loud little handful--as usual--will shout for the war. The pulpit will--warily and cautiously-- object--at first; the great, big, dull bulk of the nation will rub its sleepy eyes and try to make out why there should be a war, and will say, earnestly and indignantly, 'It is unjust and dishonorable, and there is no necessity for it.' Then the handful will shout louder. A few fair men on the other side will argue and reason against the war with speech and pen, and at first will have a hearing and be applauded; but it will not last long; those others will outshout them, and presently the anti-war audiences will thin out and lose popularity. Before long you will see this curious thing: the speakers stoned from the platform, and free speech strangled by hordes of furious men who in their secret hearts are still at one with those stoned speakers--as earlier--but do not dare say so. And now the whole nation--pulpit and all--will take up the war-cry, and shout itself hoarse, and mob any honest man who ventures to open his mouth; and presently such mouths will cease to open. Next the statesmen will invent cheap lies, putting the blame upon the nation that is attacked, and every man will be glad of those conscience-soothing falsities, and will diligently study them, and refuse to examine any refutations of them; and thus he will by and by convince himself the war is just, and will thank God for the better sleep he enjoys after this process of grotesque self-deception.

There is a charm about the forbidden that makes it unspeakably desirable.

There is no character, howsoever good and fine, but it can be destroyed by ridicule, howsoever poor and witless. Observe the ass, for instance: his character is about perfect, he is the choicest spirit among all the humbler animals, yet see what ridicule has brought him to. Instead of feeling complimented when we are called an ass, we are left in doubt.

There is no sadder sight than a young pessimist, except an old optimist.

There is no such thing as a new idea. It is impossible. We simply take a lot of old ideas and put them into a sort of mental kaleidoscope. We give them a turn and they make new and curious combinations. We keep on turning and making new combinations indefinitely; but they are the same old pieces of colored glass that have been in use through all the ages.

There is nothing so annoying as having two people talking when you're busy interrupting.

There is something fascinating about science. One gets such wholesale returns of conjecture out of such a trifling investment of fact.

There isn't time, so brief is life, for bickerings, apologies, heartburnings, callings to account. There is only time for loving, and but an instant, so to speak, for that.

There was never yet an uninteresting life. Such a thing is an impossibility. Inside of the dullest exterior there is a drama, a comedy, and a tragedy.

There were two Reigns of Terror, if we would but remember it and consider it; the one wrought murder in hot passion, the other in heartless cold blood; the one lasted mere months, the other had lasted a thousand years; the one inflicted death upon ten thousand persons, the other upon a hundred millions; but our shudders are all for the horrors of the minor Terror, the momentary Terror, so to speak; whereas, what is the horror of swift death by the axe, compared with lifelong death from hunger, cold, insult, cruelty, and heart-break? What is swift death by lightning compared with death by slow fire at the stake? A city cemetery could contain the coffins filled by that brief Terror which we have all been so diligently taught to shiver at and mourn over; but all France could hardly contain the coffins filled by that older and real Terror—that unspeakably bitter and awful Terror which none of us has been taught to see in its vastness or pity as it deserves.

There's one way to find out if a man is honest: ask him; if he says yes, you know he's crooked.

They did not know it was impossible so they did it.

They said they would rather be outlaws a year in Sherwood Forest than President of the United States forever.

Those who don't read good books have no advantage over those who can't.

Thunder is good, thunder is impressive; but it is lightning that does the work.

To a man with a hammer, everything looks like a nail.

To be, or not to be; that is the bare bodkin
That makes calamity of so long life;

To believe yourself brave is to be brave; it is the one only
essential thing.

To do good is noble. To tell others to do good is even nobler
and much less trouble.

To get the full value of joy you must have someone to divide
it with.

To me [Edgar Allan Poe's] prose is unreadable—like Jane Austin's. No there is a difference. I could read his prose on salary, but not Jane's. Jane is entirely impossible. It seems a great pity that they allowed her to die a natural death.

To place man properly at the present time, he stands somewhere between the angels and the French.

Tom said to himself that it was not such a hollow world, after all. He had discovered a great law of human action, without knowing it -- namely, that in order to make a man or a boy covet a thing, it is only necessary to make the thing difficult to attain. If he had been a great and wise philosopher, like the writer of this book, he would now have comprehended that Work consists of whatever a body is obliged to do, and that Play consists of whatever a body is not obliged to do. And this would help him to understand why constructing artificial flowers or performing on a tread-mill is work, while rolling ten-pins or climbing Mont Blanc is only amusement. There are wealthy gentlemen in England who drive four-horse passenger-coaches twenty or thirty miles on a daily line, in the summer, because the privilege costs them considerable money; but if they were offered wages for the service, that would turn it into work and then they would resign.

Too much of anything is bad, but too much good whiskey is barely enough.

Training is everything. The peach was once a bitter almond; cauliflower is nothing but cabbage with a college education.

Travel is fatal to prejudice, bigotry, and narrow-mindedness, and many of our people need it sorely on these accounts. Broad, wholesome, charitable views of men and things cannot be acquired by vegetating in one little corner of the earth all one's lifetime.

Truth is stranger than fiction, but it is because Fiction is obliged to stick to possibilities; Truth isn't.

Unconsciously we all have a standard by which we measure other men, and if we examine closely we find that this standard is a very simple one, and is this: we admire them, we envy them, for great qualities we ourselves lack. Hero worship consists in just that. Our heroes are men who do things which we recognize, with regret, and sometimes with a secret shame, that we cannot do. We find not much in ourselves to admire, we are always privately wanting to be like somebody else. If everybody was satisfied with himself, there would be no heroes.

Under certain circumstances, profanity provides a relief denied even to prayer.

Use the right word, not its second cousin.

We have a criminal jury system which is superior to any in the world and it's efficiency is only marred by the difficulty of finding twelve men every day who don't know anything and can't read-

We may not pay Satan reverence, for that would be indiscreet, but we can at least respect his talents.

We should be careful to get out of an experience only the wisdom that is in it and stop there lest we be like the cat that sits down on a hot stove lid. She will never sit down on a hot stove lid again and that is well but also she will never sit down on a cold one anymore.

Well, everybody does it that way, Huck.
Tom, I am not everybody.

What a wee little part of a person's life are his acts and his words! His real life is led in his head, and is known to none but himself. All day long, the mill of his brain is grinding, and his thoughts, not those of other things, are his history. These are his life, and they are not written. Everyday would make a whole book of 80,000 words -- 365 books a year. Biographies are but the clothes and buttons of the man -- the biography of the man himself cannot be written.

What gets us into trouble is not what we don't know. It's what we know for sure that just ain't so.

What is joy without sorrow? What is success without failure? What is a win without a loss? What is health without illness? You have to experience each if you are to appreciate the other. there is always going to be suffering. It's how you look at your suffering, how you deal with it, that will define you.

What is Man? Man is a noisome bacillus whom Our Heavenly Father created because he was disappointed in the monkey.

What work I have done I have done because it has been play. If it had been work I shouldn't have done it. . . . The work that is really a man's own work is play and not work at all. . . . When we talk about the great workers of the world we really mean the great players of the world.

What would men be without women? Scarce, sir...mighty scarce.

What's the use you learning to do right when it's troublesome to do right and ain't no trouble to do wrong, and the wages is just the same?

When a man loves cats, I am his friend and comrade, without further introduction.

When angry, count four. When very angry, swear.

When I am king they shall not have bread and shelter only, but also teachings out of books, for a full belly is little worth where the mind is starved.

When I was a boy of 14, my father was so ignorant I could hardly stand to have the old man around. But when I got to be 21, I was astonished at how much the old man had learned in seven years.

When I was younger, I could remember anything, whether it had happened or not; but my faculties are decaying now and soon I shall be so I cannot remember any but the things that never happened. It is sad to go to pieces like this but we all have to do it.

When ill luck begins, it does not come in sprinkles, but in showers.

When in doubt tell the truth. It will confound your enemies and astound your friends.

When people do not respect us we are sharply offended; yet deep down in his private heart no man much respects himself.

When red-headed people are above a certain social grade their hair is auburn.

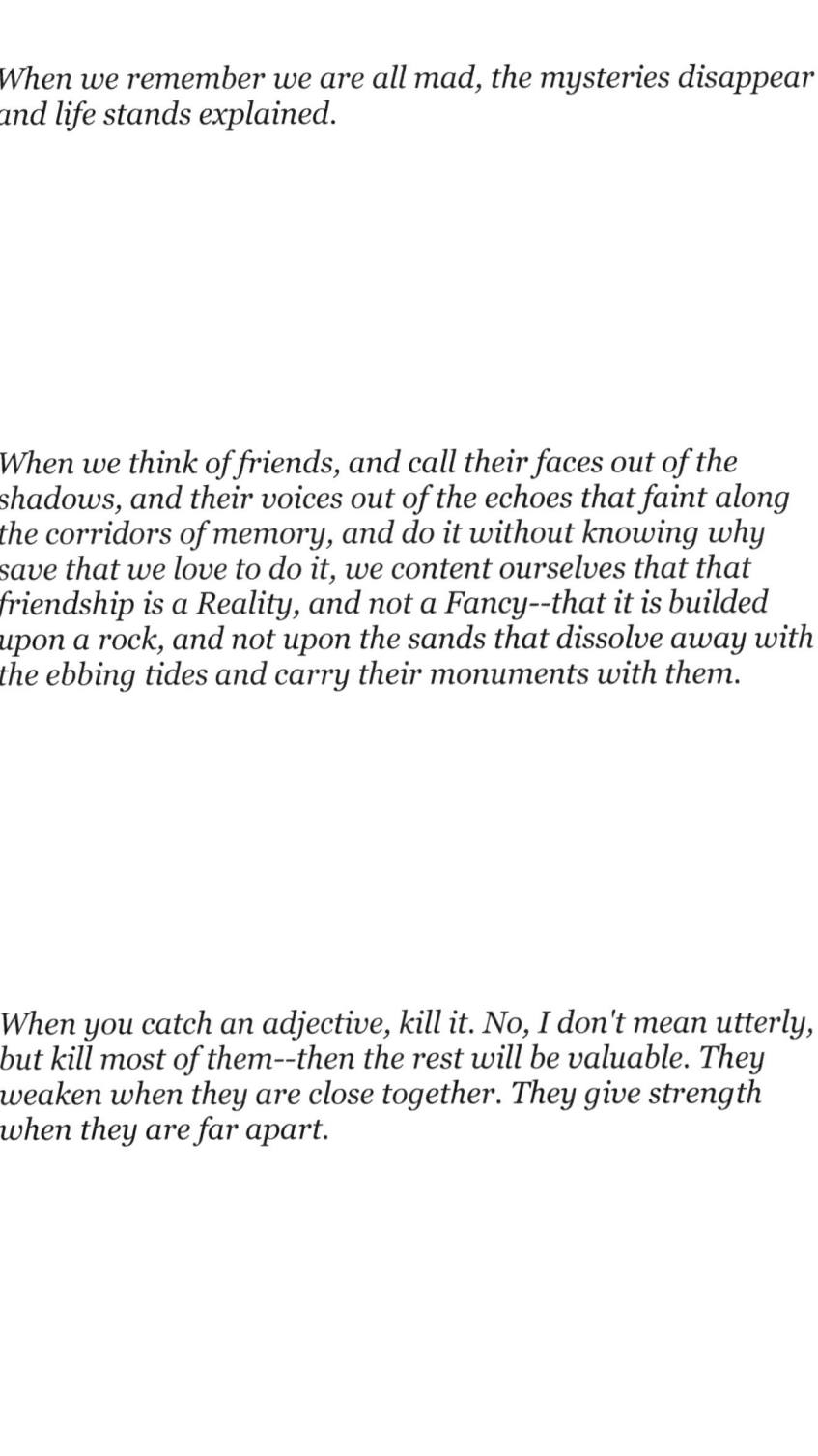

When we remember we are all mad, the mysteries disappear and life stands explained.

When we think of friends, and call their faces out of the shadows, and their voices out of the echoes that faint along the corridors of memory, and do it without knowing why save that we love to do it, we content ourselves that that friendship is a Reality, and not a Fancy--that it is builded upon a rock, and not upon the sands that dissolve away with the ebbing tides and carry their monuments with them.

When you catch an adjective, kill it. No, I don't mean utterly, but kill most of them--then the rest will be valuable. They weaken when they are close together. They give strength when they are far apart.

When you fish for love, bait with your heart, not your brain.

Whenever the literary German dives into a sentence, this is the last you are going to see of him till he emerges on the other side of his Atlantic with his verb in his mouth.

Whenever you find yourself on the side of the majority, it is time to reform (or pause and reflect).

Wheresoever she was, there was Eden.

While the rest of the species is descended from apes, redheads are descended from cats.

Whiskey is for drinking; water is for fighting over.

Who knows, he may grow up to be President someday, unless they hang him first!

Whoever is happy will make others happy too.

Why do you sit there looking like an envelope without any address on it?

Why is it that we rejoice at a birth and grieve at a funeral? It is because we are not the person involved.

Will a day come when the race will detect the funniness of these juvenilities and laugh at them—and by laughing at them destroy them? For your race, in its poverty, has unquestionably one really effective weapon—laughter. Power, Money, Persuasion, Supplication, Persecution--these can lift at a colossal humbug,—push it a little— crowd it a little—weaken it a little, century by century: but only Laughter can blow it to rags and atoms at a blast. Against the assault of Laughter nothing can stand.

Wit is the sudden marriage of ideas which before their union were not perceived to have any relation.

Words are only painted fire, a look is the fire itself. She gave that look, and carried it away to the treasury of heaven, where all things that are divine belong.

Work like you don't need the money. Dance like no one is watching. And love like you've never been hurt.

Worrying is like paying a debt you don't owe.

Wrinkles should merely indicate where the smiles have been.

Write what you know.

Write without pay until somebody offers to pay.

Writing is easy. All you have to do is cross out the wrong words.

You are not you--you have no body, no blood, no bones, you are but a thought. I myself have no existence; I am but a dream--your dream, a creature of your imagination. In a moment you will have realized this, then you will banish me from your visions and I shall dissolve into the nothingness out of which you made me. I am perishing already, I am failing, I am passing away.

In a little while you will be alone in shoreless space, to wander its limitless solitudes without friend or comrade forever—for you will remain a thought, the only existent thought, and by your nature inextinguishable, indestructible. But I, your poor servant, have revealed you to yourself and set you free. Dream other dreams, and better!

Strange! that you should not have suspected years ago— centuries, ages, eons, ago!—for you have existed, companionless, through all the eternities.

Strange, indeed, that you should not have suspected that your universe and its contents were only dreams, visions, fiction! Strange, because they are so frankly and hysterically insane—like all dreams: a God who could make good children as easily as bad, yet preferred to make bad ones; who could have made every one of them happy, yet never made a single happy one; who made them prize their bitter life, yet stingily cut it short; who gave his angels eternal happiness unearned, yet required his other children to earn it; who gave his angels painless lives, yet cursed his other children with biting miseries and maladies of mind and body; who mouths justice and invented hell—mouths mercy and invented hell—mouths Golden Rules, and forgiveness multiplied by seventy times seven, and invented hell; who mouths morals to other people and has none himself; who frowns upon crimes, yet commits them all; who created man without invitation, then tries to shuffle the responsibility for man's acts upon man, instead of honorably placing it where it belongs, upon himself; and finally, with altogether divine obtuseness, invites this poor, abused slave to worship him!

You perceive, now, that these things are all impossible except in a dream. You perceive that they are pure and puerile insanities, the silly creations of an imagination that is not conscious of its freaks—in a word, that they are a dream, and you the maker of it. The dream-marks are all present; you should have recognized them earlier.

It is true, that which I have revealed to you; there is no God, no universe, no human race, no earthly life, no heaven, no hell. It is all a dream—a grotesque and foolish dream. Nothing exists but you. And you are but a thought—a vagrant thought, a useless thought, a homeless thought, wandering forlorn among the empty eternities!

You believe in a book that has talking animals, wizards, witches, demons, sticks turning into snakes, burning bushes, food falling from the sky, people walking on water, and all sorts of magical, absurd and primitive stories, and you say that we are the ones that need help?

You can't depend on your eyes when your imagination is out of focus.

You can't pray a lie -- I found that out.

You can't reason with your heart; it has its own laws, and thumps about things which the intellect scorns.

You can't throw too much style into a miracle.

You meet people who forget you. You forget people you meet. But sometimes you meet those people you can't forget. Those are your 'friends

www.ingramcontent.com/pod-product-compliance
Lightning Source LLC
Chambersburg PA
CBHW070911100726
47907CB00008B/2277